Here, boy!

HAVE YOU SEEN MY

First edition 2023

Library of Congress Catalog Card Number 2022907291
ISBN 978-1-5362-2625-6

23 24 25 26 27 28 CCP 10 9 8 7 6 5 4 3 2 1

Printed in Shenzhen, Guangdong, China

This book was typeset in Vision.
The illustrations were done in mixed media.

Candlewick Press
99 Dover Street
Somerville, Massachusetts 02144

www.candlewick.com

INVISIBLE DINOSAUR?

Helen Yoon

CANDLEWICK PRESS

I'm looking for my invisible dinosaur.
Have you seen him? He's about this tall.

Maybe taller.

See, he had gotten REALLY dirty,
so I had to give him a big, BIG bath.
I soaped him and scrubbed him
and rinsed him until he was
extra clean.

mud

←Dinosaur

me

bubles

Extra, EXTRA clean.

That's when I lost him.

Uh-oh.

I thought making his favorite snack
would help him find his way back.

But that didn't work.

I tried putting up *Lost Dinosaur* posters.

That didn't work, either.

Sigh.

If only it were raining.

Then I'd find him easy-peasy.

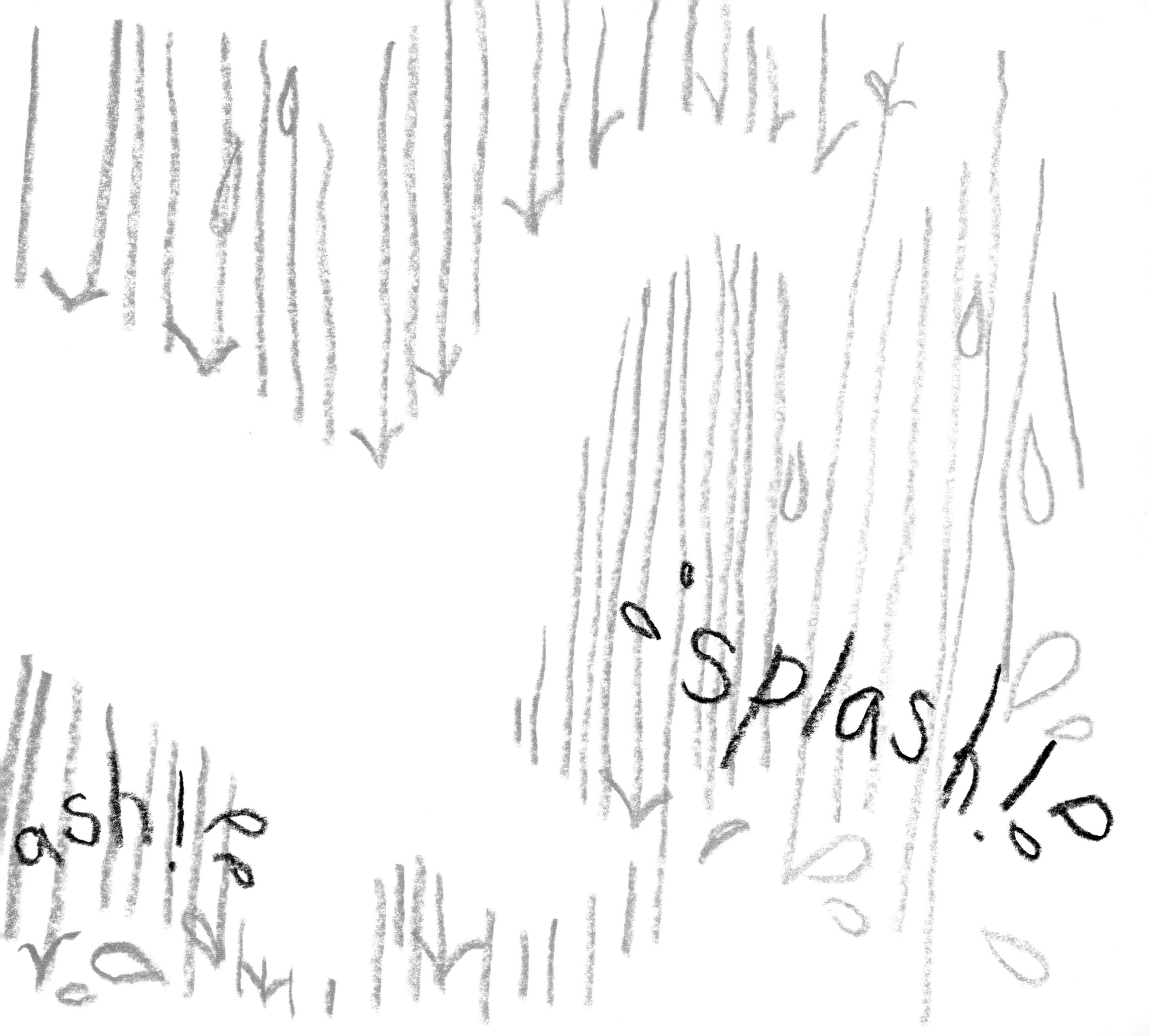
ash!
splash!

Or snowing.

crunch
crunch
crunch

Or anything, really.

But on a pretty and sunny day,
like today?

Nothing.

Hm?

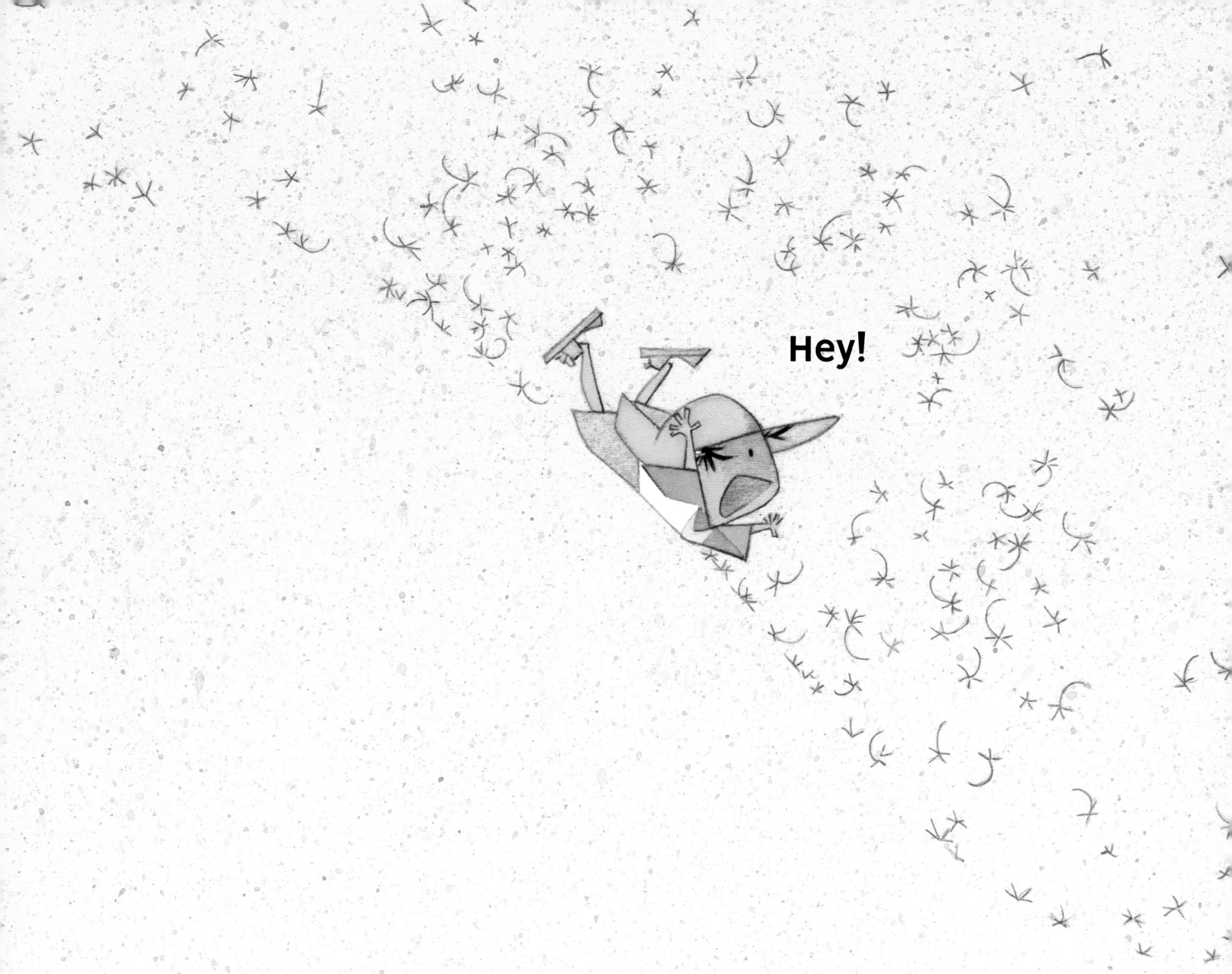
Hey!

There you are!

munch,
munch,
munch!

You found me!

Oh boy, you need
another bath.